KEEPING YOUR COOL

by Michael Scotto
illustrated by The Ink Circle

STARRING

BROADWAY
WANNADOGOOD
The Theater Owner
& Playwright

Broadway owned the Portal
Theater in Midlandia. At his theater,
Broadway wrote and directed plays
for everyone to enjoy.

Broadway kept a close eye on every detail of his plays. He had to be sure that everything turned out just how he wanted. "I loved the way you said that line, Beaker," he said. "However, try it again, just a touch more quietly. That will be much more dramatic."

Everyone tried to do exactly as Broadway said, because if they did not...

"No, no, no!" Broadway hollered. "That was too slow! I said a little slower, not slow like a turtle! I can't believe this!"

Broadway had an awful temper. "Nobody ever listens!"
he cried, stomping his feet. **"It's a tragedy!** It could
make a Midlandian weep. In fact, that's just what I'll do!"

After Broadway had calmed down, he noticed
that his tummy was grumbling. "Boy, all that jumping
around made me hungry!" he thought.

Broadway decided to stop for his favorite snack:
a blueberry muffin at his friend Bun's bakery.

Broadway reached the counter. "One blueberry muffin, please!" he said.

Bun gulped nervously. "I'm sorry, Broadway," he stammered. "I just sold my last one."

Broadway could not believe his ears! "You're out of blueberry muffins?" he asked.

Bun nodded nervously. He knew that when Broadway lost his temper, he could be very tough to handle. "If you like...I do have some banana muffins," Bun suggested. "Perhaps you might enjoy something new."

That really got Broadway steamed. He felt his face getting hot. **"But I didn't come for something new!"** he yelled.

Meanwhile, Harmony watched from her table. She was a musician, and Broadway let her play shows at his theater.

"Uh-oh..." Harmony whispered. She knew what was coming next.

In the blink of an eye, Broadway jumped onto the counter and started toppling things over like an angry whirlwind. "I just want my blueberry muffin!" he howled. **"This is a tragedy!"**

As Broadway stamped his feet, he felt a hand touch his ankle. It was Harmony! "Can we go somewhere and talk?" she asked.

Harmony and Broadway sat together in the park.
Broadway was no longer mad—he was worried.
"Oh, gracious, I was really rude to Bun," he said.
"I am so embarrassed."

"Why do you think you got so upset?" asked Harmony.
"I just get so frustrated when things don't go my way,"
Broadway replied. "I try not to get upset, but I feel like I
can never hold my temper in!"

"Everybody feels upset, or disappointed, or even angry sometimes. But losing your temper is never a good idea. It can be scary, and it is hurtful to others," Harmony said. "Would you like to know how I keep my cool?"

"I would love to know," Broadway replied.

"When I think I might lose my temper," Harmony said, "I like to count to ten. It gives me time to calm down."

"I don't know, Harmony," Broadway said. "With my temper, I might need to count to a million. Do you have any other ideas?"

"How about this?" Harmony said. "When I'm upset, sometimes it helps me to think of things that make me laugh or smile. What makes you smile?"

"I always smile when I think about my theater," Broadway said. "After each show, I get to come out and take a bow. Everybody claps for me!"

"If you thought about that, there's no way you could stay angry!" Harmony said.

"Maybe you're right," Broadway replied doubtfully.

"I also have one more solution you can try," Harmony
said. "Instead of trying to hold your temper in, you could
use it to do something creative!"

"I've heard of losing your temper, but I've never heard
of using your temper," Broadway said. "How can I do that?"

"Sometimes," Harmony said,
"I dance to music! Or, I'll take out my banjo and make up a song."

"I'm not very good at dancing or singing," Broadway said. "Could I write a story or a play instead?"

"**Good thinking!**" Harmony exclaimed. "You could write your feelings down, or you could draw a picture about them."

"Maybe I'll write my next big hit!" Broadway said.
"Thanks for helping me, Harmony. I should go apologize to Bun."

As Broadway waited in line to apologize, he began to feel frustrated. "One, two, three, four..." he whispered to himself. As he counted, the line moved along. Soon, it was his turn to talk with Bun.

"I'm so sorry for losing my temper with you," Broadway told Bun. "It was not fair to treat you that way. From now on, I'll try to be a little more patient and kind. Can we still be friends?"

"**Friends**," Bun replied, and he shook Broadway's hand.
"Good!" Broadway said. "Because the next time I have a new play opening, there will be a front row ticket waiting for you!"
From that day on, Broadway always tried to control his temper. He counted, he hummed songs, he thought of funny things...

He even wrote a new play.

Keeping his cool was very hard work. But as you can see, it gave Broadway plenty to smile about.

DISCUSSION QUESTIONS

Have you ever felt frustrated? What made you feel that way? How did you handle it?

Can you think of any more ways to deal with being in a bad mood?